A NOTE TO PARENTS

One of the most important ways children learn to read — and learn to *like* reading — is by being with readers. Every time you read aloud, read along, or listen to your child read, you are providing the support that she or he needs as an emerging reader.

Disney's First Readers were created to make that reading time fun for you and your child. Each book in this series features characters that most children already recognize from popular Disney films. The familiarity and appeal of these high-interest characters will draw emerging readers easily into the story and at the same time support basic literacy skills, such as understanding that print has meaning, connecting oral language to written language, and developing cueing systems. And because Disney's First Readers are highly visual, children have another tool to help in understanding the text. This makes early reading a comfortable, confident experience — exactly what emerging readers need to become successful, fluent readers.

Read to Your Child

Here are a few hints to make early reading enjoyable and educational:

★ Talk with children before reading. Let them see how much they already know about the Disney characters. If they are unfamiliar with the movie basis of a book, take a few minutes to look at the cover and some of the illustrations to establish a context. Talking is important, since oral language precedes and supports reading.

★ Run your finger along the text to show that the words carry the story. Let your child read along if she or he recognizes that there are repeated words or phrases.

★ Encourage questions. A child's questions are good clues to his or her comprehension or thinking strategies.

★ Be prepared to read the same book several times. Children will develop ease with the story and concepts, so that later they can concentrate on reading and language.

Let Your Child Read to You

You are your child's best audience, so encourage her or him to read aloud to you often. And:

★ If children ask about an unknown word, give it to them. Don't interrupt the flow of reading to have them sound it out. However, if children start to sound out a word, let them.

★ Praise all reading efforts warmly and often!

— Patricia Koppman
Past President
International Reading Association

Layouts by Judie Clarke
Pencils by Denise Shimabukuro and Scott Tilley
Paintings by Atelier Philippe Harchy

ISBN 0-590-39389-8

12 11 10 9 8 7 6 5 4 3   8 9/9 0 1 2 3/0

Printed in the U.S.A.   23

First Scholastic printing, May 1998

This book is set in 20-point New Aster.

Mulan Saves the Day

Adapted by Nancy E. Krulik
Illustrated by Atelier Philippe Harchy

Disney's First Readers — Level 1
A Story from Disney's *Mulan*

SCHOLASTIC INC.
New York Toronto London Auckland Sydney

There is a war in China.
Mulan's father can't fight.
So she pretends to be a man,
to go in her father's place.

Mulan rides to the army camp.
Mushu the dragon goes with her.

Mulan meets Captain Shang.
It is his job to train the new soldiers.

Mulan tries hard.
But she makes many mistakes.
Big mistakes!

The soldiers must climb a tall pole.
All the soldiers fail many times.
Finally, Mulan makes it to the top!

The enemy attacks!
Can Mulan and her friends
stop the Huns?

Clever Mulan aims the cannon
at the mountain.
Snow covers the Huns. Hooray!

But Captain Shang is in trouble.
Mulan must pull him to safety.

Mulan is the bravest one of all.
But the men find out
that she is a woman.
They leave her alone
on the mountain.
And Mulan sees that the
Huns still live.

She must warn
the Chinese army!
Once in the city,
Mulan uses her brain
to save the Emperor.

Mulan comes home a hero.
She has saved China and brought
honor to her family.